KT-546-725

HOPSCOTCH
TWISTY TALES

Mole Versus the Enormous Turnip

by Dawn Casey

and Michael Emmerson

FRANKLIN WATTS
LONDON•SYDNEY

This story is based on the traditional fairy tale,
The Enormous Turnip, but with a new twist.
You can read the original story in
Hopscotch Fairy Tales. Can you make
up your own twist for the story?

Franklin Watts
First published in Great Britain in 2015 by The Watts Publishing Group

Text © Dawn Casey 2015
Illustrations © Michael Emmerson 2015

The rights of Dawn Casey to be identified as the author
and Michael Emmerson as the illustrator of this Work have been asserted
in accordance with the Copyright, Designs and Patents Act, 1988.

All rights reserved.

ISBN 978 1 4451 4299 9 (hbk)
ISBN 978 1 4451 4300 2 (pbk)
ISBN 978 1 4451 4308 8 (library ebook)

Series Editor: Melanie Palmer
Series Advisor: Catherine Glavina
Series Designer: Peter Scoulding
Cover Designer: Cathryn Gilbert

Printed in China

Franklin Watts
An imprint of
Hachette Children's Group
Part of The Watts Publishing Group
Carmelite House
50 Victoria Embankment
London EC4Y 0DZ

An Hachette UK Company
www.hachette.co.uk

www.franklinwatts.co.uk

MIX
Paper from
responsible sources
FSC® C104740

Mole lived in a snug little hole.

Above the ground, the farmer
was planting seeds.

One turnip seed grew bigger
and bigger and bigger.

Mole's home got smaller and smaller and smaller.

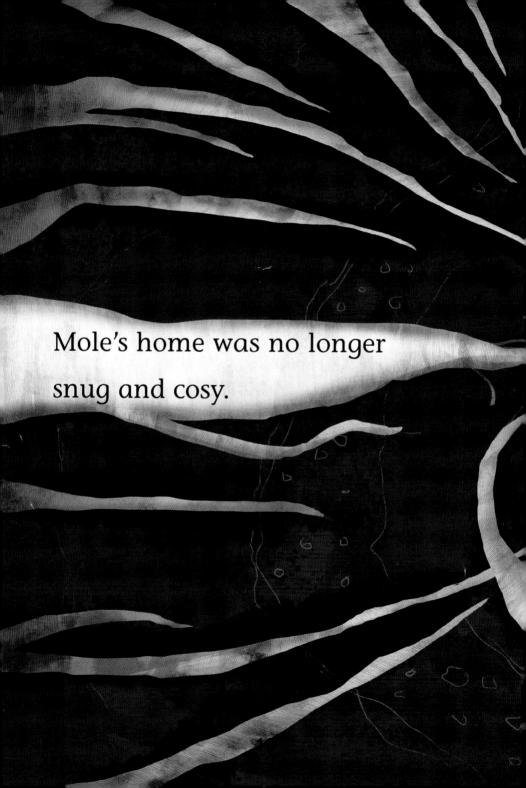

Mole's home was no longer
snug and cosy.

It was squashed and squished.

"I'll sort this out," said Mole.

He rolled up his sleeves,

bent his knees and PUSHED.

But the turnip did not move.

Mole called to Badger. "Badger! Come and help me to push up this enormous turnip!"

Badger pushed Mole and Mole
pushed the enormous turnip.
But the turnip did not move.

Badger called to Rabbit. "Rabbit! Come and help us to push up this enormous turnip!"

Rabbit pushed Badger and Badger
pushed Mole and Mole pushed the
enormous turnip. But the turnip
did not move.

Rabbit called to Beetle. "Beetle! Come and help us to push up this enormous turnip!"

Beetle pushed Rabbit and
Rabbit pushed Badger and
Badger pushed Mole and Mole
pushed the enormous turnip.

POP!

Out flew

the turnip.

The farmer *was* surprised!

"Thank you," said the farmer.
"I was wondering how to get
that turnip up."

"Never mind your turnip,"
cried Mole. "Look at my home!"

"Oh!" said the farmer. "I'll help you." So the farmer worked with his spade.

And the farmer's wife worked with her needle and thread.

Badger, Rabbit and Beetle all
helped Mole.

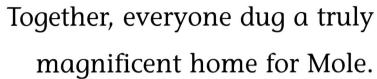

Together, everyone dug a truly
magnificent home for Mole.

Mole's new home was so big
he could invite all his friends
for a feast!

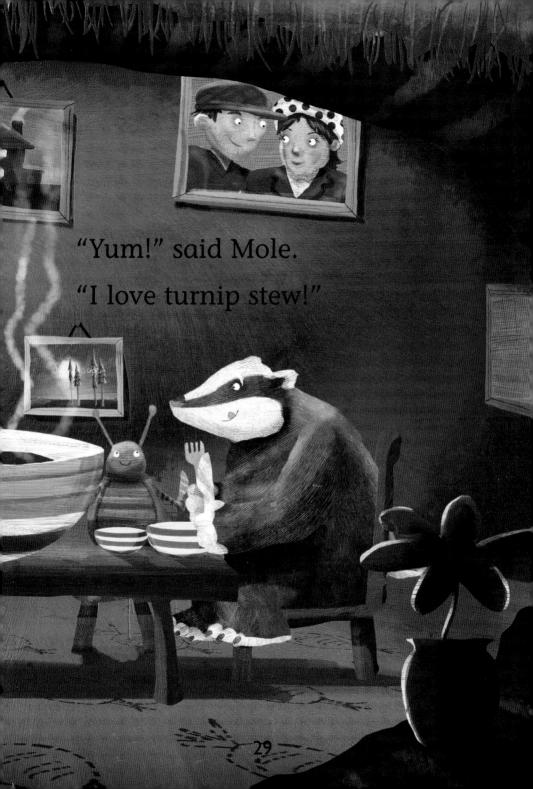

"Yum!" said Mole.

"I love turnip stew!"

Puzzle 1

Put these pictures in the correct order.
Which event do you think is most important?
Now try writing the story in your own words!

Puzzle 2

Choose the correct speech bubbles for each character. Can you think of any others? Turn over to find the answers.

Answers

Puzzle 1

The correct order is: 1c, 2e, 3f, 4b, 5d, 6a

Puzzle 2

Mole: 1, 5

The farmer: 2, 3

Badger: 4, 6

Look out for more Hopscotch Twisty Tales and Fairy Tales:

TWISTY TALES
The Lovely Duckling
ISBN 978 1 4451 1633 4
Hansel and Gretel and the Green Witch
ISBN 978 1 4451 1634 1
The Emperor's New Kit
ISBN 978 1 4451 1635 8
Rapunzel and the Prince of Pop
ISBN 978 1 4451 1636 5
Dick Whittington Gets on his Bike
ISBN 978 1 4451 1637 2
The Pied Piper and the Wrong Song
ISBN 978 1 4451 1638 9
The Princess and the Frozen Peas
ISBN 978 1 4451 0675 5
Snow White Sees the Light
ISBN 978 1 4451 0676 2

The Elves and the Trendy Shoes
ISBN 978 1 4451 0678 6
The Three Frilly Goats Fluff
ISBN 978 1 4451 0677 9
Princess Frog
ISBN 978 1 4451 0679 3

Rumpled Stilton Skin
ISBN 978 1 4451 0680 9
Jack and the Bean Pie
ISBN 978 1 4451 0182 8
Brownilocks and the Three Bowls of Cornflakes
ISBN 978 1 4451 0183 5
Cinderella's Big Foot
ISBN 978 1 4451 0184 2
Little Bad Riding Hood
ISBN 978 1 4451 0185 9
Sleeping Beauty – 100 Years Later
ISBN 978 1 4451 0186 6

FAIRY TALES
The Three Little Pigs
ISBN 978 0 7496 7905 7
Little Red Riding Hood
ISBN 978 0 7496 7907 1
Goldilocks and the Three Bears
ISBN 978 0 7496 7903 3
Hansel and Gretel
ISBN 978 0 7496 7904 0
Rapunzel
ISBN 978 0 7496 7906 4
Rumpelstiltskin
ISBN 978 0 7496 7908 8
The Elves and the Shoemaker
ISBN 978 0 7496 8543 0
The Ugly Duckling
ISBN 978 0 7496 8544 7

Sleeping Beauty
ISBN 978 0 7496 8545 4
The Frog Prince
ISBN 978 0 7496 8546 1
The Princess and the Pea
ISBN 978 0 7496 8547 8
Dick Whittington
ISBN 978 0 7496 8548 5
Cinderella
ISBN 978 0 7496 7417 5
Snow White
ISBN 978 0 7496 7418 2
The Pied Piper of Hamelin
ISBN 978 0 7496 7419 9
Jack and the Beanstalk
ISBN 978 0 7496 7422 9
The Three Billy Goats Gruff
ISBN 978 0 7496 7420 5
The Emperor's New Clothes
ISBN 978 0 7496 7421 2